SHELLRAISER

MIKEY'S HOT ROD

SERVICE TRUCK

T-MACHINES
TURBO GUIDE

T-MACHINES
TURBO GUIDE

© Viacom International Inc.

T-MACHINES
TURBO GUIDE

© Viacom International Inc.

T-MACHINES
TURBO GUIDE

© Viacom International Inc.

nickelodeon

TEENAGE MUTANT NINJA TURTLES™
T-MACHINES
TURBO GUIDE

Illustrated by Patrick Spaziante

A Random House PICTUREBACK® Book

Random House 🏠 New York

© 2015 Viacom International Inc. and Viacom Overseas Holdings C.V. All rights reserved. Published in the United States by Random House Children's Books, a division of Penguin Random House LLC, 1745 Broadway, New York, NY 10019, and in Canada by Random House of Canada, a division of Penguin Random House Ltd., Toronto. Pictureback, Random House, and the Random House colophon are registered trademarks of Penguin Random House LLC. Nickelodeon, Teenage Mutant Ninja Turtles, and all related titles, logos, and characters are trademarks of Viacom International Inc. and Viacom Overseas Holdings C.V. Based on characters created by Peter Laird and Kevin Eastman.
randomhousekids.com
ISBN 978-0-553-53867-0
Printed in the United States of America
10 9 8 7 6 5 4 3 2 1

SHREDDERMOBILE

Shredder's newest criminal creation is the Shreddermobile. This fuel-injected mean machine has an engine created by the Kraang and is protected by heavy-duty armor. Like its driver, the Shreddermobile is fast, powerful, and full of tricks—it fires steel daggers, and its wheels have retractable spikes that can shred a rival's tires.

SHELLRAISER

To battle Shredder's automotive monsters, Donnie has scavenged metal and machine parts and created a fleet of super vehicles for his brothers and friends. The Shellraiser is the Turtles' ultimate armored assault vehicle. Salvaged from an old subway car, it is armed with a trash cannon and a manhole-cover launcher.

AT-3

This three-wheeled all-terrain vehicle is nimble and powerful. Its twin engines give Leo the speed he needs to lead any attack. And the reinforced tires mean he can take this bike anywhere—off road, through the sewer, and over roofs!

MIKEY'S HOT ROD

Made for speed but hard to control, Mikey's muscle car is perfect for the silliest Turtle. It's equipped with a smoke-bomb launcher and a reinforced grille, which can bash through doors and walls. The rear bed is perfect for carrying pizza boxes—it's warmed by the eight exhaust pipes.

This tow truck with attitude is Donnie's garage on wheels. It can haul away wrecks and allows Donnie to make repairs on the run. Powered by recycled pizza oil, it has real green power!

RAT ATTACK

Like the sensei himself, Splinter's lowrider is stylish and stealthy. It's not flashy, but when cornered, it has a few tricks under its hood.

ICE MACHINE

The Ice Machine is perfect for a rink warrior like Casey Jones. The front features a defense-shattering snowplow that shoots hockey pucks, while the back lays down super-slick sheets of ice to freeze enemies in their tracks.

SHELLCRUSHER

Fishface's Shellcrusher slides through the streets like a deep-sea nightmare. Its razor-sharp fins give it a quick turning radius, and it can drop fish-oil slicks to give the Turtles the slip.

THE SAFARI TRUCK

Tiger Claw's Safari Truck is perfect for off-road Turtle hunting. The steel-studded tires tear up the streets, while the front and back net launchers snag unlucky prey.

When darkness falls, the Turtles and their T-Machines are ready to burn rubber and keep the streets safe.

RAT ATTACK

ICE MACHINE

SHELLCRUSHER

THE SAFARI TRUCK